Also by Claude Clément:
The Painter and the Wild Swans

Also by John Howe:
Jack and the Beanstalk
Rip van Winkle

Copyright © 1989 by Editions Duculot
English text based on a translation by Fiona M. Gaskin

First U.S. Edition 1990

Library of Congress Catalog Card Number 89-84593

ISBN: 0-316-14740-0

10 9 8 7 6 5 4 3 2 1

First published in 1989 in Belgium by Editions Duculot

Printed in Belgium

WRITTEN BY CLAUDE CLÉMENT

MUSICIAN FROM THE DARKNESS

ILLUSTRATED BY JOHN HOWE

Little, Brown and Company   Boston Toronto London

This happened long ago, far back in the mists of time,
even before mankind began to speak.

Before the dawn's first rays entered the cave, the man with sky-blue eyes got up and raked life back into the dying embers on the hearth.

The others, their limbs still stiff with cold and sleep, sat up from where they had slept.

The women hitched their young onto their backs and were the first to go out to gather the wild fruit that hung from the bushes covered with red blossoms. They dug in the damp earth in search of tender roots.

The men prepared their tools and weapons. They kept at their side a young boy whom they were going to initiate into the ways of the hunt.

At the entrance of the cave the man with the sky-blue eyes stood staring at the sun as it burnished the crest of the hills. While the others went on ahead, his features softened, and he raised his arms as if to hail the sun. The boy watched him and waited behind so that he could walk at the man's side. Together they hurried and caught up with the other men of the tribe.

At a turning in the path the men split into two groups. The strongest, those armed with the heaviest weapons, went in pursuit of big game. The others, who were armed only with small javelins and slings, went toward the ponds and marshes.

They hid there in the tall grasses and they saw a flock of birds land on the water. But the birds were too far away for the hunters to reach with their spears and stones.

The man with the sky-blue eyes
seemed ill at ease as hunter.
Instead he listened to the calls
of the birds and the fluttering
of their wings. He listened to the
sighing of the wind in the reeds.
Then, slicing a stem with a piece
of sharpened flint, he made a
coarse flute and raised it to his
lips. He blew a few notes through
it in imitation of the birds' song.

Deceived by these tones,
some of the birds flew toward
the hunters. The men pierced
them with their weapons and
rushed after them over the
watery grassland.

As the surviving birds called out to each other in warning, the blood from those killed slowly stained the reeds in front of the man with the blue eyes.

The hunters waited for their companion to lift the flute to his lips again. But he stayed motionless and the remaining birds flew away.

The men from the tribe shouted angrily at the silent man. They chased him away into the marsh and would not let him return to the cave with them. They motioned for the boy to go with them and he did, pausing sometimes to look behind him.

Alone and without any way of
starting a fire, the man with the
sky-blue eyes watched anxiously
as night fell.

For a long time he lay on the
ground, listening in terror as the
distant cries of animals broke
the silence. Gradually he saw a
strange light that glimmered on
the surface of the water. The
moon was rising and pushing
back the edges of the night.

He realized that in his trembling
fingers he still held the flute.
Slowly, he sat up and began
to play.

The dark night was filled with
the sounds he made.

Amazed by his own playing,
he began inventing sounds and
rhythms that resembled the
cries of animals, the creaking
of branches, or the sound of the
wind in the reeds.

The man played on, and not long before the sun rose, he noticed that the boy had returned and was watching him, listening.

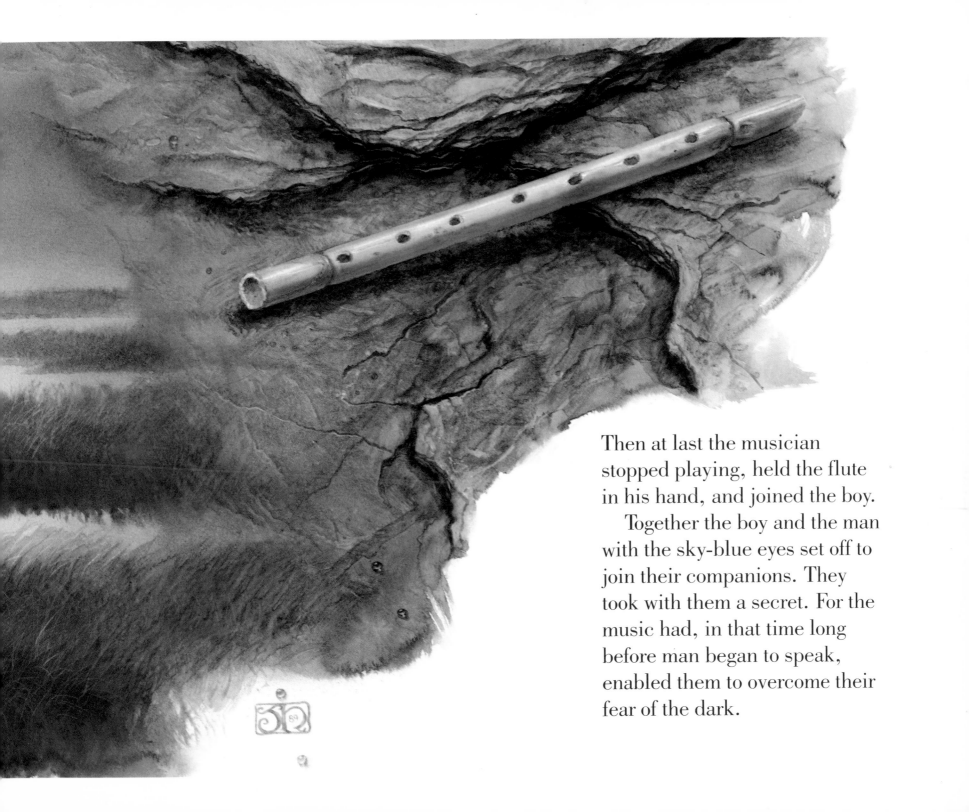

Then at last the musician stopped playing, held the flute in his hand, and joined the boy.

Together the boy and the man with the sky-blue eyes set off to join their companions. They took with them a secret. For the music had, in that time long before man began to speak, enabled them to overcome their fear of the dark.